Beowulf

A Hero's Tale Retold

by James Rumford

Houghton Mifflin Company
Boston 2007

What you have heard before is nothing. I will stir up the waters of the old days and shape the long-ago then into now. I will speak of ogres and dragons and faraway lands. Listen! for I will sing of Beowulf, a man bold and fearless, and tell you the truth about hard-won fights and steadfast hearts.

In the dragon marshes of Denmark there lived an ogre. His name was Grendel.

He hated the Danes and their king Hrothgar [ROTH-GAR]. He couldn't stand to hear them drinking and laughing in the great king's hall while he lay in the cold water by the sea.

Dark night after dark night, Grendel broke into the hall called Heorot [HAY-OH-ROT] and ate his fill of Hrothgar's men. No one could stop him, and grim dawn after grim dawn, Denmark mourned.

Twelve winters went by, and Hrothgar grew old and weary under this evil. Word of Grendel spread far and wide.

A young man, a bold man, in the land of the Geats [YEETS], swore an oath to help the Danish king.

As reckless as this oath was, no one dared stop the young man, for he was strong-willed and fire-hearted, keen to be known throughout the world for great deeds.

He readied a boat and asked fourteen friends to go with him. Together, boldly, daringly, they sailed over the wide whale sea to Denmark.

As soon as they landed, a lookout called, "Who goes there?"

"We are Geats and have come in friendship," answered the young man. "Tell us, is it true about the ogre?"

"It is true. All Denmark lives in fear."

"Then take us to your king, for we have come to stop this evil."

The lookout led the Geats, their boar-headed helmets gleaming in the sun, to Heorot. Halfway up the hill, where the old wooden gods stood, one of Hrothgar's men stopped them.

"Who are you to come helmet-and-spear to the great king's hall?"

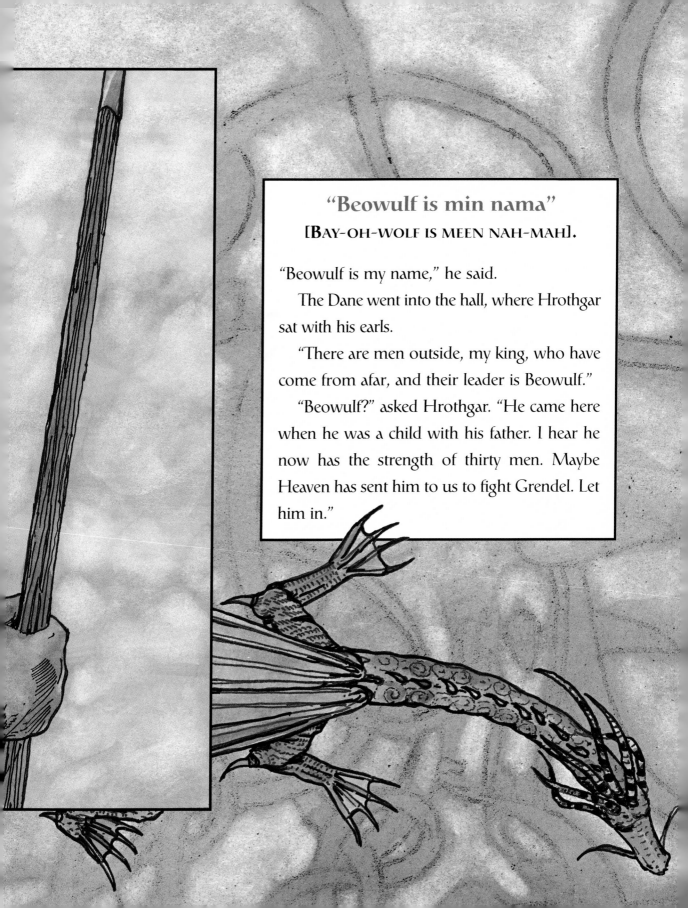

"Beowulf is min nama"
[BAY-OH-WOLF IS MEEN NAH-MAH].

"Beowulf is my name," he said.

The Dane went into the hall, where Hrothgar sat with his earls.

"There are men outside, my king, who have come from afar, and their leader is Beowulf."

"Beowulf?" asked Hrothgar. "He came here when he was a child with his father. I hear he now has the strength of thirty men. Maybe Heaven has sent him to us to fight Grendel. Let him in."

The great doors opened and Beowulf went inside, his helmet and iron shirt gleaming even in the dark hall.

"Hail, Hrothgar! I, son of Ecgetheow [EDGE-THEY-OH], have done great deeds. I stand before you this day ready to fight Grendel."

The old king's eyes widened. "Once your father came for help and I gave it to him. For this he swore an oath of friendship. Since he is no more, you have come to make good his word and help us in our time of need. For this, we are thankful. As for Grendel, he will be here soon enough, and we shall see what you can do. But now come, sit with us."

Beowulf bowed, and the king called for food and drink. Soon the hall was filled with talk of the coming fight. Even the queen came and spoke, wishing Beowulf and his friends well.

But at twilight, the Danes left. Only the Geats and his men dared sleep in the hall.

"Since Grendel wields no weapon, neither shall I," Beowulf told his men. "Let the outcome of this fight be up to wise God."

And the darkening hall drew in the night.

When sleep was at its deepest, night at its blackest, up from the mist-filled marsh came Grendel stalking.

He burst through the great hall doors and sent the iron bolts flying. He wrenched a man from his sleep and swallowed him in clumps.

Then he reached for Beowulf! But Beowulf was ready and grasped the ogre's arm.

Grendel roared and writhed and wrestled to free himself from Beowulf's locklike grip. The two hammered into the walls. They broke benches and sent the drinking cups flying.

All the while, Beowulf's men hacked at Grendel with their swords. Their blades could not harm him, though, for the ogre had weakened their weapons with a mighty spell. But he had no spell over Beowulf's iron grip.

A deep wound now opened up on Grendel's shoulder and widened. The sinews were bursting, the arm bones loosening.

There was only one way out. The ogre tore himself free and ran one-armed into the night!

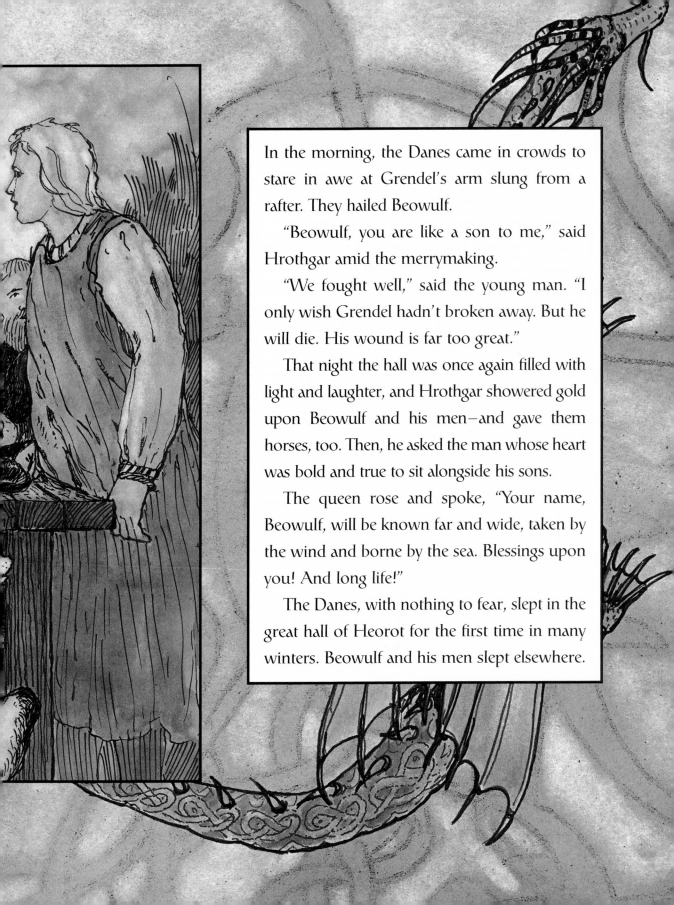

In the morning, the Danes came in crowds to stare in awe at Grendel's arm slung from a rafter. They hailed Beowulf.

"Beowulf, you are like a son to me," said Hrothgar amid the merrymaking.

"We fought well," said the young man. "I only wish Grendel hadn't broken away. But he will die. His wound is far too great."

That night the hall was once again filled with light and laughter, and Hrothgar showered gold upon Beowulf and his men—and gave them horses, too. Then, he asked the man whose heart was bold and true to sit alongside his sons.

The queen rose and spoke, "Your name, Beowulf, will be known far and wide, taken by the wind and borne by the sea. Blessings upon you! And long life!"

The Danes, with nothing to fear, slept in the great hall of Heorot for the first time in many winters. Beowulf and his men slept elsewhere.

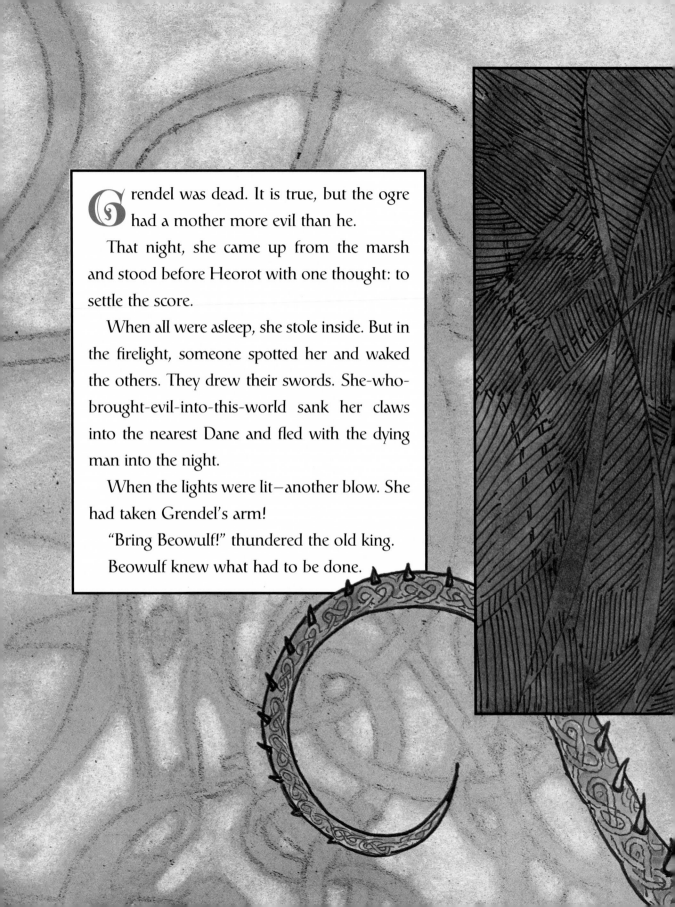

Grendel was dead. It is true, but the ogre had a mother more evil than he.

That night, she came up from the marsh and stood before Heorot with one thought: to settle the score.

When all were asleep, she stole inside. But in the firelight, someone spotted her and waked the others. They drew their swords. She-who-brought-evil-into-this-world sank her claws into the nearest Dane and fled with the dying man into the night.

When the lights were lit—another blow. She had taken Grendel's arm!

"Bring Beowulf!" thundered the old king.

Beowulf knew what had to be done.

At dawn, Beowulf led his men—and Hrothgar's,
too—down to the marsh, following a bloody
path.

At the first loud blast from the king's horns,
dragons hiding in the cliffs dove into the water.

Beowulf stood at the edge of the marsh and
donned his shirt of woven iron and helmet of
beaten gold.

"Look after my men if I don't come back,"
he told Hrothgar before sliding down into the
dark water.

It took Beowulf half a day to reach the bottom. There Grendel's mother was watching.

In a whoosh she was on him, sticking her sharp claws into his iron-woven shirt.

When she could not break through to his flesh, she let her dragons tear at him with their tusks and teeth and claws.

Beowulf withstood them all, and, one by one, they swam away.

The mouth of the hag's lair—made so that no water seeped inside—beckoned.

He went in.

A fire blazed inside. In its glow stood Grendel's mother, in all her might.

Beowulf swung his sword. It sang out as it struck her head, but the blade did nothing to her, for she had weakened his weapon with a spell. But Beowulf had one weapon she could not weaken: his bare hands. He took hold of her and threw her to the ground.

She sprang back up. She knocked him off his feet and swooped down with her knife for the kill. But the blade could not bite through the iron shirt to the flesh. Beowulf leapt up.

A gleaming on the wall drew his eye. It was a sword—a giant's sword hanging there with the old hag's other weapons. He gripped the heavy blade and swung with all his might. Steel met flesh, killing her in one blow.

Beowulf looked around. There, lifeless on the bed, was Grendel. He swung the giant's sword once again, hacking off the ogre's head.

Blood spewed out everywhere, and from it the blade of the giant's sword began to melt. When those on the bank saw the reddening water, they feared the worst. Hrothgar left with his men, taking hope with him. Beowulf's men now stood alone, helpless, before the churning marsh.

Then up through the gore-red waves came Beowulf, unharmed!

His men ran to help him out of the water. With high hearts, they went back to Heorot, bearing the ogre's giant head. Reaching the hall, they boldly strode inside.

"Hail, Hrothgar," called Beowulf, holding high the hilt of the giant's sword. "Let what is left of this sword be a token of my deeds, for I have done what I said I would do."

"You have been true to your word," said the king. "Soon the world will know your name."

The throng in the hall grew loud, hailing Beowulf and their king.

Hrothgar held his hand up to still the crowd and speak the wisdom of his years: "Do not climb so high, good Beowulf, that you forget who you are: a man under Heaven among brothers. Share all you have in your hand and heart. Give freely. Now, come, let us eat and drink."

Beowulf took his seat amid the merry-making. When all had eaten and drunk their fill, the cowl of night came over the land and well-earned sleep to all.

"Caw! Caw!" It was the morning raven, calling Beowulf to gather his men and bid farewell to Hrothgar.

The king gave twelve chests of gold and gems to Beowulf, and he kissed him as a father would a son. Then he broke down in tears, knowing that, as old as he was, he would never see his friend again. Beowulf, now shining with gold, took his men down the hill to the wave-weaving sea and home.

When Beowulf reached the land of the Geats, he went to his king, Hygelac [HYOOG-GUH-LACK], to tell him of his deeds. As Hygelac and his earls listened, they saw Beowulf not as they had before, a careless youth, but as a man heart-strong and true.

Then, as is the way of great men, Beowulf gave everything the Danes had given him to his king. Hygelac called for his gem-studded sword and bestowed it upon Beowulf. He gave him land too, and a great hall. All was well.

The years flew by.

Hygelac died and his son after him. Beowulf became king of the Geats, and he was loved by all.

Fifty winters came and went. Beowulf was now old with frost-white hair. He drank mead with his friends and listened to the song tales of bygone days, the gold-shining days of his youth. But the mead and the songs were only a stillness before the storm.

"A dragon!" the Geats wailed.

"A flying fire-snake," they cried, "has come to our land!"

For three hundred years this dragon had slept in a lair beneath the earth, watching over a hoard of gold and gems. Then one day, someone found a way in and stole a golden drinking cup, only that. The dragon awoke and, full of hate, flew out of its lair, burning and killing, making ashes even of Beowulf's hall.

The old king knew what had to be done.

Beowulf called for the smith to make an iron shield to withstand the dragon's fire and asked for his sword, which had never once let him down in a fight.

When all was ready, he chose a band of eleven men to go with him. Then he had the wretch who had stolen the cup brought in.

"This is all your doing!" roared Beowulf. "For this wrong, you will take us to where the dragon lives."

Frightened, the quaking man led the king and his men to the cliffs by the sea and showed them the dark hole in the earth.

Beowulf stopped. Inside this lair was the dragon that threatened to sweep all away and take him, too. Though worn and torn from years of fighting, the king said, "I may be old, but I will end this evil myself or die fighting."

Then Beowulf went to the lair alone, calling, daring the fire-worm to show itself.

Slithering and unwinding, the dragon worked its fiery way forward. It reared up and blasted Beowulf, who held fast to his iron shield even as the molten breath came roaring over him.

Then, amid the heat and smoke, Beowulf struck hard with his sword. But the blade wouldn't go in.

The dragon rose higher and higher and smothered him in a blaze of fire. Beowulf was doomed.

When his band of men saw this, they fled for their lives. One man, Wiglaf by name, stopped.

"We can't leave him to die! We have to go back!"

"He said he'd do it alone," the others answered. "Let him."

"Better to burn than leave a friend in need," Wiglaf said.

Wiglaf headed into the smoke, calling, "My king! I shall stand by you."

When the dragon saw Wiglaf, it blasted him, making ashes of his wooden shield.

Seeing Wiglaf gave Beowulf new strength, and he ran his sword into the dragon. This time the blade went through the shining hornlike hide right to the flesh. Then—*crack*—the sword that had never let him down broke in two!

The dragon, now wounded and writhing, sank its fangs into Beowulf's neck.

It was then that Wiglaf showed his true heart-strength. Shieldless, with seared hands, he stuck his gleaming sword into the dragon. This freed Beowulf, who drew a knife from his belt and buried it deep inside the fire-snake.

The dragon reared up and fell over, dead.

Then Beowulf fell.

The bite on Beowulf's neck began to swell and burn from the dragon's deadly spit.

Wiglaf found water and bathed the wound with his fire-blackened hands.

Beowulf spoke, even as dark death flowed inside him: "Wiglaf, I have no sons, so I give all to you. As for the gold, gather it up. But quick!"

Wiglaf ran into the lair and gathered what he could. He laid the gold before his dying lord.

Beowulf opened his eyes, old eyes full of sorrow. "I thank Heaven that I did not back down—not once. When I am dead, have my body burned, as is our way. Heap up a high hill on the cliff for all to see."

Then he gave Wiglaf what a father would give his son, his neck ring and helmet worked with gold.

"You are the last of my kinsmen. The rest have all gone," he said, "swept away by Heaven's will."

Then came his last words:

"Ic him æfter sceal"
[ICH HIM AFTER SHALE].

"I must follow them."

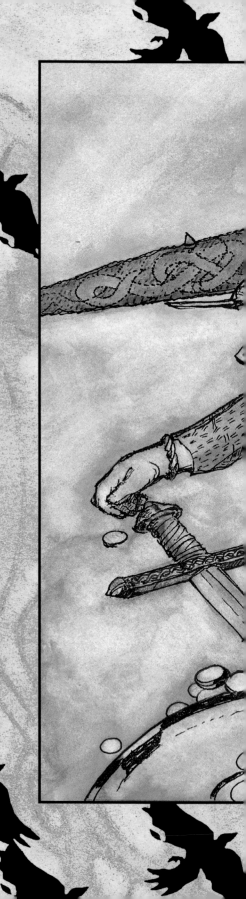

The others now came out of hiding, bearing their shields and their everlasting shame.

They found Wiglaf holding Beowulf.

"You!" Wiglaf said amid his tears. "Where were you? I could do little alone. Our king would still be alive had you been here."

The news went out. Beowulf was dead, and Wiglaf stood lordless and heart-heavy before a heap of gold. Then Wiglaf told the men to bring out all the hard-earned wealth. As it lay gleaming in the sunlight, they shoved the fire-worm's body over the cliff.

On a headland, the Geats heaped up wood and laid their lord on top. They lit a fire and wept, as bright heaven swallowed the smoke. A woman came forward singing a sorrow-song— of the foes who would come upon them like ravens, like wolves, now that Beowulf was gone.

Of the ashes they built a hill and hid deep inside the dragon's wealth—all of it. There it lies to this day, beyond our reach now as ever it was.

Then they gave thanks for Beowulf. Once he said a thing, he kept his word. Once he set his mind, he never backed down. Steadfast, right-hearted, to the end.

Now let the old waters be still and the long-ago days go back to the deep. This tale of Beowulf, a man loved by all and keen to make great his name, is ended.

Beowulf is a hero poem. Over several centuries, the poets or scops (pronounced "shopes"), as they were called then, recited the tale from generation to generation. About the year A.D. 800, someone, perhaps a Christian monk, wrote the poem down in Old English or Anglo-Saxon, the ancient language that forms the basis of the English we speak today.

Who were the speakers of that language? They were the Angles and the Saxons. They came from Germany and Denmark and invaded Britain more than 1,500 years ago. They called their new country England, Land of the Angles. They ruled the land for almost six hundred years.

Then in 1066, everything changed. A French-speaking king named William conquered England. The English began using French words. Over the next three hundred years, the language lost thousands of English words as people began borrowing from French. By 1300, few people could read the ancient books, and a poem like *Beowulf* was forgotten.

But in the 1700s, scholars became interested in Old English. They rediscovered the ancient stories and retold them in Modern English. It was at that time that they found the only surviving manuscript of *Beowulf*. In 1832, it was published for all to appreciate.

So what remains of Anglo-Saxon? A lot, for from it come our common, everyday words—powerful, straightforward words that form the backbone of our language.

What are these words? To give you an idea, I have retold the story of Beowulf using just those words that can be traced back to the ancient language. Some of my words come from Latin and Greek, like *dragon, ogre,* and *giant,* but I thought this was all right since they were already part of Anglo-Saxon. And three words, *they, their,* and *them,* are not Anglo-Saxon at all but come from Old Norse, the language of the Vikings. I found I couldn't tell the story without them.

The study of the origin of words is called etymology, and any good English dictionary will lay out the word-saga of our language for you to explore. There are also modern retellings of *Beowulf.* But prepare yourself, for the ancient words will make the night darker, the shadows deeper, and, perhaps, your heart bolder.

www.houghtonmifflinbooks.com

In writing this book, the author relied upon the original text of the poem *Beowulf* as well as many critical essays and modern translations of the poem. He also acknowledges the recent work of Seamus Heaney, whose translation was a source of inspiration. The illustrations were inspired by the work of Arthur Rackham and Edmond Dulac and were done in pen and ink and finished with watercolor. The illumination was inspired by the Anglo-Saxon and Keltic manuscripts of the first millennium.

The text of this book is set in Catull.
Book design by Bob Kosturko

Library of Congress Cataloging-in-Publication Data

Rumford, James, 1948-
Beowulf, a hero's tale retold / by James Rumford.
p. cm.
Summary: An illustrated retelling of the exploits of the Anglo-Saxon warrior, Beowulf, and how he came to defeat the monster Grendel, Grendel's mother, and a dragon that threatened the kingdom.
ISBN-13: 978-0-618-75637-7 (hardcover) ISBN-10: 0-618-75637-X (hardcover)
1. Beowulf–Adaptations–Juvenile literature. [1. Beowulf. 2. Folklore–England.] I. Beowulf. English. II. Title.
PZ8.1.R8572Beo 2007 [398.2] dc22 2006026084

Printed in Singapore
TWP 10 9 8 7 6 5 4 3 2 1